Holding On

Holding On

Diana Engel

Marshall Cavendish   New York

Marshall Cavendish, 99 White Plains Road, Tarrytown, NY 10591

Library of Congress Cataloging-in-Publication Data
Engel, Diana.
Holding on / Diana Engel.
p.   cm.
Summary: Twelve-year-old Thomas, who likes to draw, is dismayed when his
mother leaves him with his eccentric great-uncle Tano for an extended visit,
until the two of them explore the natural world around the isolated house
and work together on a stained glass panel.
ISBN)-7614-5016-5
[1. Great-uncles—Fiction. 2. Artists—Fiction.] I. Title.
PZ7.E69874Ho   1997   [Fic]—dc21   96-45635   CIP   AC

The text of this book is set in 12 point Berling.
Book design by Constance Ftera

Printed in the United States of America

1   3   5   7   8   6   4   2

*This book is dedicated to the memory of
my Uncle Tommy (Gaetano Magistro) . . . and
to my great friend, Roni Schotter, who convinced me
that I had a story worth telling*

Chapter 1

They raced along in the bright sunlight, passing cars of every color with stupid messages on their license plates and bumpers.

Thomas sat in the front seat, furious and silent. He was held tight by the seatbelt, which dug under his earlobe and wrapped diagonally across his chest.

Thomas felt like a prisoner . . . a prisoner going off to jail.

His mother couldn't stop talking. While she drove, she chattered on, trying to convince her scowling, dark-haired son that he would have a good time.

"My uncle's really okay," she said, "and he's got all kinds of interesting stuff. You'll like him. I know it."

Thomas hated his mother's uncle or at least the little he remembered of him. They had visited two years ago when Thomas was ten. It was a short visit, barely an hour, but Thomas remembered Uncle Tano. He could close his eyes now and see the skinny old man staring at him. He could feel Uncle Tano's hard, prickly cheek pressed against his own. And most of all, he could smell the cat pee.

"His house stinks!" said Thomas, spitting out each word and hoping they would hurt his mother's feelings.

Two weeks! He thought. *Two solid weeks in that smelly, old house . . . my whole Easter break!*

Thomas had wanted to stay with his best friend, Luke. Just thinking about Luke made him smile. Luke's family was big, and noisy, and terrific. They rented movies on Friday nights and ate Chinese food in the living room all together—four kids and two adults passing the egg rolls and yelling at each other to keep quiet.

Thomas often wished he was the fifth child in Luke's family—so much activity, so many plans, and so much freedom from being in the spotlight. Not like at his house. It was just he and his mother, and she focused all her laser-beam attention on him. Thomas loved his mother with equal intensity, but sometimes he needed a break from being the center of her life. Thomas could picture the vacation at Luke's: glowing and open, full of fresh air and possibilities.

Instead, he and his mother were on their way to Connecticut from their home in Baltimore. There had been many discussions but, in the end, Thomas's mother had insisted that while she visited her own sick mother in a nursing home in Boston, Thomas would stay with her Uncle Tano. The old man had actually asked her, she said. Thomas couldn't picture that happening and thought his mother had probably made it up. She was always smoothing things over, making things nice. Thomas thought he preferred the ugly truth.

The trip was long and boring and it got worse by

the minute. Thomas's anger coiled in him like a snake as he thought of the two weeks ahead. He saw a dark tunnel, pressing at him on all sides.

"His house stinks!"

Thomas said it again, this time turning, watching his mother's reaction. Her sad eyes met his and then quickly glazed in self-defense. A split second later, she was focused on the highway before her.

"Let's just stop for a quick bite," she said, scanning the signs on the Jersey Turnpike.

"I'm not hungry," mumbled Thomas, staring straight ahead.

"Well, I need a stretch," said his mother, "so I'll get us some stuff for the rest of the ride."

The car slowed and turned into the parking lot of a non-descript restaurant.

Thomas unhooked the seatbelt, rubbed his ear, and watched the kids tumble happily out of the cars around him. He knew what it felt like to run free from a car towards the greasy treats waiting beyond the doors of a truck stop diner. Thomas's stomach rumbled. Eventually, his mother returned with a bag of food, napkins and straws peeking from the top. "Buckle up," she said, as she dug around for ketchup.

Amidst the smells of fries and hot dogs, Thomas tried to sit quietly. *"I will not eat!"* he told himself. He clenched his jaws and concentrated his anger. Maybe his mother would feel the rays of rage he was sending her way.

She only smiled, wiping ketchup smears from the

side of her mouth. "You'll be fine, Hon," she said. "Uncle Tano's a little strange, but he can be fun, too. You know, I used to spend a lot of time with him. He was really like a father to me. Come on, Sweetie, have a fry."

Thomas's own father was somewhere in Texas. At least that was what his mother said. His parents had been divorced for about a year but, even before, they hadn't been together much.

"Your father's not bad," his mother told him on the day of the divorce. "He's just . . . ," she looked somewhere in the distance to find the right words. "He's just not capable of having a family . . . of the commitment . . . the everyday . . . the small things. He just can't do it. I don't know why. He tried."

Her words stopped and began again. "And look how little time he spent here! Always running off for weeks . . . I just couldn't take it anymore," she said. "I just couldn't."

Thomas had looked at his mother's tired face. It was true, he thought. His father had been in and out of their lives, always returning with armloads of presents and big plans for the future, but never staying long enough to make Thomas feel it was for good. It wore him down, checking each morning to see if his father lay sleeping in the bed next to his mother. Or running home from school only to find the familiar disappointing note in his father's scrawl: "Be back soon, Buckaroo. Love you."

Yet Thomas had held on tightly to the crazy hope

that things would change. Even after his mother had given up, he clung to the shreds of his past, revisiting those thoughts that would keep his father a presence in his life.

Thomas had sharp, clear memories of nearly all of the times he and his father had been together. Most of the memories had to do with hands. He didn't know why, but they did . . . strong hands, warm hands, big man's hands. They held Thomas's memories of his father somewhere safe within him. Some were vivid pictures, like the trip to Lucky's Hardware on that busy corner downtown. His father had let Thomas pick out a shiny ball peen hammer with a smooth wooden handle. Thomas had carried it home, happily aware of the pull of the heavy metal in his hand and of the heavy hand of his father, resting lightly on his shoulder.

Other memories were only snatches, moments of feelings: of being lifted, lifted, swung into the air, held by a strong web of fingers while the world blurred, until he sat snug on his father's shoulders like a sailor in a crow's nest, safe and high above the heads of all others moving below.

Thomas savored these and other memories and saw them stretching back through his life like a beaded necklace, each bead a different memory separated from the next by a long length of time.

Now, instead of visits, he received letters. Sometimes the letter folded around a check for his mother. She vowed she would never take his father's help, but

Thomas knew that she had no choice and that she quietly added the money to her small salary.

Once, his father sent a photograph which had been taken before Thomas was born. It was a picture of his father and mother sitting side by side at the dining room table. His father's arm hung protectively on the back of his mother's chair, and their faces glowed in the light from birthday candles before them. His parents were smiling. On the back of the picture, his father had written: "Thought you might like this."

Thomas had stared at the image for a long time, trying to picture the celebration. Why had his father sent it to him? Was it a secret message? Did his father still love his mother? Maybe it was just the opposite. Maybe his father hated her so much that he couldn't stand to keep her picture. The worst message Thomas imagined was that before he was born, his mother and father were truly happy. Maybe, thought Thomas, he had been the one to ruin things for them!

Thomas hid the photo in his sock drawer. For some reason, he wanted to hold onto it, even if it confused him. He liked the way the candles lit the happy young faces. Sometimes, when he looked at the picture, the word "family" seemed less lonely.

Often at night, if he couldn't fall asleep, Thomas made up family vacations. He imagined vivid trips he and his mom and his dad had taken. He might begin one, fall asleep before it ended, and add more details the next night.

He could see them so clearly. In one vacation, the family was scuba diving in turquoise water, swimming past bright orange coral reefs. They held hands and kicked their flippers in unison. He even saw the air bubbles dancing around them as they laughed at the schools of parrot fish darting and turning.

Thomas keep these images with him. In the last year, he had begun to draw them in a private notebook he kept under his mattress. He spent hours trying to match his sketches to his nighttime visions.

His favorite vacation was a trip across the Yukon. Thomas could see himself sitting in a dog sled, wrapped in caribou hides and his mother's arms. His father guided the dog team from behind, slicing the air with a huge whip, shouting "Mush!" to the panting huskies. Thomas could feel the cold and see his own breath. And though he had few memories of it, he was sure that the feelings of warmth and safety he had imagined were exactly the way it would be if his family were together.

"Come on, Honey," said his mother, "I'm sure you're starving. Eat something."

Thomas crunched his face and narrowed his eyes, staring straight ahead. He hated his father now for not being able to take him for the two weeks. But he hated his mother more, chirping and slurping in the seat next to him as they sped along the highway.

Chapter 2

By 6:00 p.m. they pulled into the driveway at the bottom of the hill behind Uncle Tano's house, which was really no more than a cabin. The small structure was painted a deep, dark red, with turquoise trim around the windows and doors. Thomas knew from his mother that the old man had built it himself from scratch.

They walked around to the front, past the Chinese maple and the forsythia ready to burst into flower. Uncle Tano had turned his property into an enormous garden. He spent most of his time pruning, and pinching, and planting, and weeding. Every shrub and plant was placed to complement the trees and to show off the waving lines of the small hills surrounding the pond which lay at the foot of the slope below the cabin. This was Tano's "masterpiece."

Thomas had heard plenty of stories about the pond. His mother's father and her Uncle Mario, now both dead, had spent weeks helping Tano one summer long ago, dredging a swamp that had been there since the days of the Indians. They cut trees, moved boulders, and removed tons of soggy soil. "It took three months," his mother said, "but it was worth it." Thomas would have loved to have been there, maybe taking a ride on the bulldozer or even scooping up mud with the backhoe. That would have been something!

Now Thomas stood near the water. He saw the rowboat and the perfect little island in the middle of the pond, no bigger than his own room at home. Two tall cedar trees stood at its center, one larger than the other, like watchmen guarding the shores, daring anyone to destroy what the men of his family had done in that long-ago summer.

The setting sun filled the water with light as a group

of noisy Canada geese flew overhead. Thomas looked up at the birds and turned to the little house above him. A picture window covered one whole side and, like the pond, seemed to be filled with gold. A screened porch perched on the right side of the house facing a rough-hewn gazebo.

It was under the gazebo, his mother had told him, that she celebrated her August birthdays when she was a child. Her family had lived in this town on the coast of Connecticut. Its few small stores faced Long Island Sound and the lumps of land offshore known as the Thimble Islands. Captain Kidd and his pirates had once sailed these waters, preying on wealthy ships that foundered on the dangerous shoals.

Thomas's mother's family was almost all gone now. His mother's mother was old and sick. She didn't even know who Thomas was anymore. Uncle Tano, her only other relative, had lived in his little house on the hill overlooking the pond for almost fifty years. Thomas had heard that the townspeople didn't like Uncle Tano. They thought he was weird and difficult. "Eccentric," his mother had said.

A movement in the window caught Thomas's eye. He saw the figure of his mother's uncle move past, ready to open the door.

"Hey!" called Tano, letting the screen door slap behind him. "Come on up!"

They trudged up the sloping hill and arrived on the terrace.

The old man looked pretty much the same as he

was in Thomas's memory: not too tall, mostly bald, with a grizzled face and sharp, blue eyes. His hands looked like tree roots, all knobby and crooked. They grabbed Thomas roughly and held him firmly by the shoulders.

"Let me look at you, young man," said Tano.

There was that stare . . . the keen eyes boring into Thomas, examining him as if he were a new species, searching for signs of value.

For a brief second, Thomas thought he would be slapped, swatted away like an ordinary bug that hadn't passed inspection.

"You look like a Castana," Tano announced and turned to hug his niece. Almost as an afterthought, he returned to Thomas and pressed his sandpaper cheek to the boy's.

Thomas searched his mother's face for some clue to her Uncle's statement.

"That's grandma's maiden name . . . before she was married," she told him. "Her family was huge and they all looked alike."

She eyed her son. He was slight and wiry. His nut-brown hair fell sideways across his forehead like a curtain opening on a stage. His eyes were the stars, dancing and dark, ringed with long lashes.

His mother laughed. "Yeah," she said, "I guess you do look like a Castana!"

"Of course he does!" said Tano loudly, waving his arm as if the mother and son were blind.

"Now get inside!" he yelled, shoving them with his booming voice and tree-root hands.

Thomas stepped through the door. There was the smell! Unmistakable. Cat pee.

But there were other smells, too: damp wood, smoky ashes, old coffee.

Thomas's memory of the room came back to him in bits and pieces.

The wooden walls were deep brown, smooth, and polished, each board fitted by hand. Somehow, the space felt churchlike—quiet and crammed with treasures.

The light from the picture window ignited the collection of antique glassware stacked on open shelves separating the tiny kitchen from the main room. Purple and green pressed glass, clear crystal, and white milk glass bowls with little nipples of bluish luminescence glowed like holiday bulbs and sent shots of color through the room.

It was a big room, filled with antiques and dominated by a gigantic stone fireplace. The mantle was one-half of a massive pine log, cut side up, bark side down, rough and intact. Animal skulls, feathers, and a collection of teacups crowded the top. Hanging above were two large oil paintings. Each was a portrait of a famous racehorse, radiantly chestnut and rippling with muscles. Though the horses faced each other, their noses were kept from touching by the heavy gilt frames that enclosed them.

Thomas's eyes roamed the room as his mother's voice chattered on. He followed the gleam from the large silver spoons hanging side by side in a wooden holder. They looked like heavy metal tongues ready to speak of times in the "Old Country"—times of thick soup and dark bread. The name "Lipari" was engraved on each handle, though Thomas didn't know what it meant.

Over the bed, which took up an alcove on the side, a ceramic face of the Madonna stared back at Thomas with wide, dark Egyptian eyes. *Can she see me?* He wondered, and hated himself for being frightened.

Books were stacked everywhere, piled in towers that threatened to fall. By the door hung a drawing of a naked man, seen from the side with his knees up, head down, an air of sadness surrounding him.

Thomas scanned it all. He looked for the familiar bulk of a television set and found none. Before despair set in, however, he was distracted by a shape in the far corner leaning towards the right: a rifle, dark and sleek, infinitely mysterious and totally interesting.

His mother's voice broke the brief silence. "Thomas has really been looking forward to staying with you, Uncle Tano." Thomas shot his mother a nasty look, but his heart wasn't in it; he was thinking about the rifle.

"Well, well," said Uncle Tano. But he was interrupted by a slapping sound coming from the porch.

In through the pet door, walked a scraggly old Siamese cat, blinking in the glare of the kitchen light.

"Beauty!" cried Tano, smiling. "Here's my Beauty!," he purred to the mangy cat. "Come here, girl, and meet my family. You were out hunting the last time they were here, weren't you, girl? Weren't you?" He picked up the cat and began nuzzling her ratty fur. Beauty tolerated the fondling for a moment and then leapt to the floor to sniff Thomas's sneakers.

"She's a beauty, all right," said Uncle Tano proudly.

Thomas smiled and thought to himself that Beauty might be the ugliest cat he had ever seen. She looked like a moth-eaten scrap of rug with skinny legs. Even her dark tail was worn and bent, sprinkled with bald spots toward the end.

When she looked at Thomas, her flat blue eyes fixed him coldly, staring like the old man's. And like the old man, she dismissed him. "Hmpf," her look

seemed to say, "you're nothing special!" Beauty trotted over to the cat box by the bathroom door and made a further contribution to the already powerful odor in the room. Thomas noticed that the box was filled not with cat litter but with shredded newspaper.

"That old girl's been around a long time," said his mother.

"And she still uses the catbox . . . never goes when she's outside?"

"Never," said Tano proudly. "Only uses the catbox, like a little lady!"

Thomas looked away and tried not to inhale too deeply.

"Oh," said his mother, touching her forehead. "I almost forgot!" She pulled a package from her massive handbag.

"I know you don't like gifts," she said looking at her uncle, "but you can always use these."

The old man opened the wrapping and saw the plastic packet marked "Fruit of the Loom." It held three pairs of white boxer shorts, tightly pressed and folded together.

"You think I'm gonna live forever?" he asked seriously.

Thomas smiled and looked down at the floor. His mother laughed.

"What?" the old man asked. "I should waste clothes like the rest of you?" His voice grew louder with each word.

"One or two pairs are good enough for me . . . wash 'em out every few days. They last for years! You people probably throw underwear away after one wearing! Disposable everything!"

Thomas's mother slapped her uncle's shoulder and kissed him lightly on the cheek.

"You are a first-class character," she said, laughing.

Thomas thought he was more than that. "Looney," he said to himself. "Looney Tunes with a cherry on top!"

Chapter 3

"Let's get some dinner together," said Tano. "The water's boiling and I made some salad."

"Here," said Thomas's mother, handing the boy a plate. Help me set the table."

They ate at the little square table in the kitchen by the window: spaghetti, salad, and chunks of home-made bread ripped off the loaf by hand.

Tano and Thomas's mother had red wine and talked through most of the meal. Sometimes their voices climbed as the conversation heated.

Thomas barely listened, trying to hold on to his earlier anger. He tried to stoke the fires by thinking how bored he was going to be in the days to come. He tried picturing himself in this smelly little kitchen with his mother's looney uncle.

Thomas noticed that Uncle Tano ate the crusts of the bread, saving the soft insides by the side of his plate.

"Just like the old days," said his mother, laughing when she, too, noticed the lumps of bread.

At the end of the meal, the old man picked up the doughy mounds he had accumulated. He crushed a few of them together in his fist, wiped his plate clean, and popped the sauce-soaked bread into his mouth. As he chewed, he began to ball the remaining bread. With one swipe, he cleaned his lips and popped this soggy clump into his mouth as well. He looked at Thomas and smiled.

"That's what I call recycling!" he said.

Thomas picked up the paper napkin by his plate and dabbed at his mouth, silent and wide-eyed.

The guy is crazy, he thought . . . *crazy!*

When the dishes were cleared and washed, the three sat in the main room drinking tea.

Uncle Tano went to a drawer and pulled out a knife, its point curiously broken off at the end. From the fridge, he brought out a large, brown slab. Thomas focused on the old man's hands and saw a gigantic chocolate bar. He had seen others like it in the supermarket, stacked in tempting piles, but his mother always whisked him past the forbidden treats before he could properly beg for one. Thomas saw the blocky silver letters shining on the front of the bar: "Hershey's Chocolate with Almonds." He pictured a pirate's chest filled to the brim with these glowing bars, each one an ingot of pure pleasure.

Now, Uncle Tano put the slab on the kitchen table. He opened the silver foil and slid back the brown paper, exposing the creamy surface of the chocolate.

Then, in a quick, violent stab, he sent the squared off tip of the knife down through the thickness of the bar, releasing a hefty chunk.

He handed this first piece to Thomas.

"My only vice," said the old man, smiling. "I never have cake or ice cream in the house, but I have to have my chocolate."

Thomas nibbled slowly at the edges of his chunk. With each swallow, a little bit of anger left him.

"Well," said his mother, sighing. "I have to get moving. I've got two more hours of driving before I get to Boston." She looked at Thomas, trying to judge his mood.

Thomas knew what she wanted from him. He had the feeling he was being used, handed over to his mother's uncle like a present. He was supposed to keep the old guy company for two weeks so his mother could feel better.

She had said it would be "good for both of them," but Thomas didn't believe a word of it.

Now, he knew she wanted a green light from him . . . a smile, a nod, a change of expression so she could walk off without guilt.

He tried to keep his face immobile. He tried to make her squirm. But it was hard. More and more he could see through his mother's cheerfulness and chatter. He could see a great tide of sadness that rose behind the flimsy fence of her words and it scared him. It scared him that he had to be strong, to keep the tide from bursting through and drowning them both.

His mother moved toward her uncle for a good-bye kiss.

"Give my love to my sister," said Tano. "Poor thing. I wish she could be put out of her misery."

"Shh," whispered Thomas's mother. "At least she's not in pain. We've got to be grateful for that."

Thomas turned toward his mother and watched her

quick movements. He knew she was trying to get out as fast as possible, but needed his small sign. He held his half-eaten chocolate in one hand and vowed to himself that whatever he did, he would not cry.

His mother bent to hug Thomas and he could see her eyes begin to redden. He reached for her and she held his dark head, crushing him against her jacket. He couldn't do it. All the anger of the previous days escaped from him, rushing out in the sobs that were muffled by his mother's hair.

"It's all right," she said softly. "It's all right."

"Aw . . . come on you two! It's only two weeks, for God's sake!" Uncle Tano's voice broke them apart.

"No crying," he said, shaking a finger at Thomas.

"He can cry if he wants to," said Thomas's mother, trying to give her son some last minute support. "Don't be too hard on him. And watch your language!" she said, glancing at her uncle. She touched Thomas's cheek and went for the door.

"Have a great time," she called over her shoulder. She didn't want another look at her son's face.

As the porch door slammed, Thomas bit into his chocolate and wolfed down the rest in two bites.

"Okay, son," said Uncle Tano, handing Thomas some sheets, "let's get your bed made up."

They arranged the pillow and blanket on the big square couch that faced the fireplace. Beauty jumped on top just as they finished.

Thomas held out his hand for the old cat, who nuzzled him gently. Then she gave his finger a quick, light nip, as if to say, "Watch out around here!"

"Ouch!" yelped Thomas, looking accusingly at his uncle.

"She doesn't mean it," said Tano. "It's her way of showing that she likes you."

"I guess I should be grateful," said Thomas, snidely, rubbing his hand.

"Well, let's go to bed," said the old man. He took off his braided leather belt, hung it on a chair and removed his shoes. Without shedding another piece of clothing, Uncle Tano lay down flat on the bed, pulled up the cover and was snoring within seconds.

Thomas was amazed. *This guy is really nuts*, he thought. *How am I gonna last two weeks?*

Through the picture window the stars twinkled. A sliver of moon shone on the pond and lit the rowboat moored on the shore.

Thomas felt very small and unable to change the course of his days. *Maybe tomorrow I can take the boat out*, he thought, *or maybe shoot at some targets in the woods. Maybe I could take the rifle in the boat and shoot out over the water.*

He climbed into his makeshift bed and set his mind on an elaborate vacation. He and his mother and father were gliding on an ancient river in a dugout canoe laden with all their belongings. They paddled past a moose nibbling grasses on the shore. Above them bald eagles soared and screeched, fish dangling from their claws . . . .

Chapter 4

Thomas awoke to a frightening sight. Beauty stood on his chest, her cold eyes investigating this unusual guest.

"Come here, girl!" called Uncle Tano, holding the cat's food dish. Beauty made a dash that left claw tracks on Thomas's chest.

"Ugh!" he grunted, sitting up, rubbing his chest, his head, his neck.

Cereal bowls and fruit were set out, and Tano was waiting at the table.

"Let's go, Tommy," he said. "We've got a lot to do around here today."

It was the first time the old man had called Thomas by name, and it wasn't the right one!

"My name is *Thomas*," he said in a flat, even tone. "I *hate* the name 'Tommy.' "

Tano's eyebrows arched up in surprise. "Well," he said, "I'm just the opposite. I hate my real name. My nickname I like."

"What's your real name?" asked Thomas, pouring milk over his cereal.

"Gaetano," the old man pronounced slowly. "Too much of a mouthful. I like Tano. Suits me better. I guess 'Thomas' suits you better than 'Tommy.' Yeah," he said looking squarely at Thomas, "I guess it does."

Thomas allowed himself a smile. He had always thought his name suited him just fine. "Tom" wasn't right and babyish "Tommy" was even worse. Ever since he was little, he had to remind people of his real name. Some people just kept right on calling him "Tommy" or "Tom" and never paid attention. He hated that. It always made him feel like he wasn't there. Like he was invisible.

Uncle Tano was up at the sink, washing the dishes. He called the boy now, putting special emphasis on the name.

"Okay, *Thomas*, let's get going!"

The old man led the way down the stone steps to the cellar. It was cool and damp, and filled with all kinds of tools, hoses, even a small tractor. There was a large worktable by the window, strewn with bits of colored glass. Long ropes of metal hung from hooks on the ceiling, like vines in an ancient forest.

"What's all that?" asked Thomas.

Uncle Tano ignored his question.

"We have to clean up the island," he said. "Getting pretty overgrown out there. . . ."

They loaded an ancient lawn mower and some clippers into the little rowboat.

"Can I row?" asked Thomas eagerly.

"No, not today," said the old man. "We've got to be quick. Maybe tomorrow."

It took a few minutes to get to the island. The surface of the water was smooth and calm. Frogs' heads appeared and disappeared as they rowed.

Thomas saw the wavy ridge of water wash over a black snake heading for shore. And all around them, under the boat, he could make out the shadowy forms of largemouth bass.

"Do you ever fish here?" he asked, thinking of another activity which might make his visit pass more quickly.

"Never!" said Tano. "I've raised these fish myself, and I'll be damned if I'll hook 'em on a line just for the fun of it!"

The rowboat bumped the edge of the island and they stepped out. They made a quick inspection and found a few old, broken egg shells.

"Damn geese," said Tano. "They nested here last year and I let them. They're beautiful, really, but they made a mess of this place. Goose poop all over the lawn. Big feathers stuck in my mower. Damn filthy mess. Then some of the little ones got eaten by the fish. I can't stand it. I won't have it . . . suffering like that on my land. This year, they're out! That's all. No more!"

"What should I do?" asked Thomas, trying to change the subject as they pulled the boat onto the island.

"Here," said Tano, handing him the clippers. "You can clean up the edges of the island . . . and over here, around the tree, too." Tano began mowing, round and round in ever smaller circles from the outer rim of the little piece of land to the center.

It was hard work for Thomas, who lay flat on his

belly trying to clip the grass right down to the water where the mower couldn't reach. *Some vacation!* He thought, *some lousy vacation!* After an hour or so, he sat down to rest, his back against the bark of the larger tree.

"We're not done yet!" said Tano sharply. "You can rest when we're finished!" The old man had taken his shirt off and Thomas took note of his firm muscles.

"I'm not your slave!" Thomas muttered back, then instantly regretted it.

The old man's face went from shock to fury. His gnarled fist was in the air threatening. "Now get up and start clipping, young man or. . . ." His words trailed off. But it was enough.

Thomas turned his back and knelt, scissoring the grass in savage, rapid movements. Tears welled in his eyes, but he kept them from brimming over. *I hate him!*, he thought. *I really* hate *him. . . . All these stupid grown ups . . . stupid, bossy grown ups . . . always telling you what to do! They don't know what they're doing half the time! I hate them all!* He snipped faster and faster as the air around him filled with clippings.

Chapter 5

When they were done, the two loaded the rowboat and stepped in. They were both silent.

Uncle Tano handed Thomas the oars. "You feel like rowing?" he asked, softly.

Thomas shook off this peace offering and turned away. His eyes settled on the shore line, where Beauty paced back and forth.

As the boat neared, Thomas could see that she had something black in her mouth and he could hear low, moaning sounds escaping her.

Uncle Tano jumped out first when the boat hit the bank.

"Bring it here, girl," he whispered. "Bring it here."

The cat approached Tano slowly, glancing up at Thomas as she passed by. She finally stopped at the old man's feet and dropped her quarry on his heavy work boot.

Thomas saw that the young starling was barely alive. A trickle of blood came from its beak and its head hung awkwardly to the side. But the breast was fluttering with rapid movements, a sign that there was still a small bit of hope.

"Watch that she doesn't touch it," said Tano gravely.

Thomas shielded the dying bird with his hands, while Beauty rubbed her head on his arms, purring.

Thomas looked up expecting to see the old man

return with a box or a towel, something to cradle the bird. Once, back home, he and his mother found a robin that had flown into their living room window and appeared dead. They had warmed it in their hands and watched it fly away. "A miracle," his mother had said. Maybe he and Tano could nurse this bird back to health too.

But when he looked up, he was horrified. Uncle Tano carried a small hatchet.

"Step away," he said. "Stay clear."

In one quick movement, he chopped the head off the bird.

"I hate to see suffering," he said. "Better to go quickly. No need to suffer. That's the way I want to go," he declared. "I'll shoot myself before I suffer like that, I really will." Then, noticing the wide-eyed silent boy, Tano took out a handkerchief and scooped up the body and head of the dead bird. "We'll bury it in a nice place, under the maple, with a view of the water," he said.

That night, the boy and the old man shared a silent dinner. Thomas was more miserable than ever. Even the big chunk of chocolate after dinner didn't comfort him. When his mother called, he felt the old anger bubble up inside him.

"Why do I have to stay here?" he asked sharply.

"Shh," said his mother, "Uncle Tano will hear you."

"I don't care," said Thomas. "I want to go home!"

"Sweetie," his mother said, "I'm sure it will get better. Please, Honey, try for me. Okay? Your grandma is pretty sick, so I can't leave her yet. Please, Hon, it won't be much longer."

Thomas felt bad that he hadn't even thought about his grandma. "All right," he muttered, feeling defeated.

Then he sat down to draw in his notebook by the picture window, where there was still a bit of light from the fading sun. Uncle Tano walked over, turned on the lamp, and watched the boy work. Ignoring him, Thomas tried to remember the way antlers sat on the head of a moose.

Tano noticed the family in the canoe: mother, father, child.

"I had no real mother or father, you know," he said, settling down opposite Thomas. "I mean, it wasn't the way it looks in your picture." The boy looked up, and from his expression, Uncle Tano knew he could go on with the story.

"My real mother and father came here a long time ago, when I was a baby. From Sicily they came . . . on a boat . . . to start a new life in America.

"When they got here, my mother *hated* it! Filthy tenements, crowded streets . . . not like the Old Country: fields, and farms, and air . . . air and sunlight!"

Thomas drew as the old man talked. Beauty lay on the arm of the couch, snoring peacefully.

"So they decided to send me back; back to my mother's aunt, who had some money but no children. She took me in as her own little bambino, and I lived with her and her husband for 10 years. Her name was Serafina Lipari . . . a beautiful woman, big and round!"

Tano was smiling, cupping his hands in the air before him, outlining an imaginary bosom. "She was something! And my uncle . . . I loved him. He was good to me, he was kind. . . . They had a farm with a lot of animals . . . goats, pigs. I loved the smell of it all. I used to lie in the barn with the baby goats . . . all afternoon, sometimes! And you know what I used to do? I would pour milk on my face so they'd lick it off with their little pink tongues!" Tano's face glowed with the memory. "I can still feel it, you know? And the olive trees . . . row after row after row," he said slowly. "The wind would blow the leaves, like silver coins, turning, turning—just like that." The old man moved his hand, palm up, palm down, back and forth in the air as he spoke. "And I'd run, I'd run through the groves, all the way from the end of the property to the big house. All hot and sweaty, I'd rush into the hallway and feel that cool air on my skin . . . see my aunt waiting for me. She'd bend her face down close to mine, and she'd wash me with a white linen towel . . . whiter than milk . . . and so cool on my forehead!"

Tano closed his eyes and lifted his head, as if the moisture of his aunt's towel still kissed his face.

Then, turning to Thomas he said, "we lived in the hills, with high mountains all around us . . . high mountains and a big volcano! Mt. Etna was always there, watching over everything, waiting to explode! Everyday, I watched her. I watched to see if she was calm or if she was boiling like the pasta pot. I thought that if I was very good, she would stay quiet, but if I was bad . . . oh boy! Then she might boil over and kill us all, with hot lava and fire!"

Like you, thought Thomas, watching the old man, *just like you! A volcano—a boiling, rumbling, unpredictable volcano!*

Tano was lost in his memories.

"Sometimes there were little explosions, but nothing as terrible as what I had imagined. But then, something else happened that was worse—something I never expected.

"One day, I ran home through the grove like I always did, but this time, the door to the house was closed. I could hear someone crying by the well. When I opened the door, more crying and stillness . . . stillness that I had never felt before.

"Someone told me my uncle had died. I think it was his heart, but in those days, who knows, it could have been something else.

"I was miserable. . . . My aunt was miserable.

"A year later, she married. I knew she didn't love that guy. I could tell. But she couldn't manage on her own. I *hated* him! He was always trying to get rid of me; always pushing his way into our lives. And he beat me. He beat me for little things, like not washing my hands or tasting the sauce in the pot. He'd beat me! My aunt tried to stop him, but he was a bully. He got his way.

"After a while, my real mother in America heard about what was going on. She wanted me to join her and the family. I cried and cried when I left my aunt. I loved her so much! I wanted to stay . . . even with the beatings, I wanted to stay. But I was sent all alone on a big ship to cross the ocean to my new home. All alone! I was a kid! Like you—a little kid! And you know what I remember from that trip?"

Thomas looked up. The old man's face was far away, gazing out over the ocean of long ago.

"I remember," said Tano "standing by the railing of the ship. I felt very small. I remember thinking that it would be so easy to fall through, down into the dark water. It was like looking into the well at home . . . only blacker and deeper, like something that never ends. I thought: *Who would hear? Who would know? I'm a little boy on a big ship! Who will take care of me now?*"

Thomas saw that the old man's eyes were full of tears. In response, his own began to sting. He saw himself being torn from the warm arms of his own mother, lost and small, floating in the blackness. He wondered if he would have survived, all alone, on that trip across the ocean.

"What happened when you got here?" he asked his great uncle.

"The boat pulled into Ellis Island in New York," said Tano. "I had to wait on long lines and get checked out by doctors. A guy from the ship helped me. I spoke only Italian.

"Then, a short man with a big black mustache came to me through the crowds. I looked up at him, like: *Who are you?* He said in Italian: *'Io sono tuo papa.'* 'I am your father.' And he took me home."

Chapter 6

Thomas woke again with Beauty on his chest, but this time she was curled up, purring contentedly. Light streamed in from the picture window and he heard birds singing loudly to the day.

"Let's go," said Uncle Tano.

"More work?" asked Thomas, expecting the worst.

"No. Today I thought we'd set up a little target practice for you." He watched the expression on the boy's face change.

"You mean it?" asked Thomas, "I can shoot the rifle?"

"Let's go!" said Tano, smiling.

The old man carried the rifle and Thomas carried the cans.

On the far side of the pond, there was a massive outcropping of granite with pink veins running through the silvery surfaces.

"There's granite all over this place," said Uncle Tano. "Beautiful stuff. They blow it out of the mountain with dynamite and cut it up into slabs. Then they send it down to New York City and who knows where, on barges. Did you know the Statue of Liberty sits on pink granite from right here where you stand? Who would've thought?" he said, shaking his head. "I end up on the same pink rock I saw when I got here as a boy! That big green lady with the torch. I was scared out of my mind! My life was a mess! Life *is* a mess! But here, here on this beautiful pink granite, I made a perfect place, eh?" Tano looked across the pond to the red cabin facing them. "Built my house on that rock," he said. "Best stone in the world. Beautiful stuff, really beautiful."

There was a low, flat rock at the edge of the larger formation. Here Thomas placed the empty cans and stepped back. Uncle Tano loaded the rifle.

"Ever shot a gun before?" he asked Thomas.

"Once," said Thomas. "A long time ago. My friend's dad took us out hunting for squirrels."

"Get one?" the old man asked.

"No," Thomas answered, "but I didn't want to. I just liked shooting the gun."

Tano nodded. "Once, I got so mad at a muskrat. It was chewing up my pond . . . the banks . . . you know . . . all around the edges . . . making holes . . . wrecking my pond. So I shot it dead in one shot. When I went to pick up its body, I found three little muskrats . . . newborns . . . I knew they'd die . . . probably get eaten by a fox or a snake. They'd never make it through the night without their mother. So I shot them, too. I felt terrible about it. I really did. That muskrat didn't know I spent my whole life making this place. I still feel bad about it. . . ." The old man's face crumpled. His eyes searched the banks, as if the ghost of the muskrat wandered there and could offer him forgiveness.

Thomas held the rifle and forced the picture of the baby muskrats out of his head. He knew he would have tried, at least, to save them.

Thomas pulled the trigger. *Bang!*

No hit. *Bang!* Again . . . *Bang!* . . . Again . . . *Bang!*

Tano knelt next to the boy and showed him how to fix the sight on the can.

"Try again," he said.

This time Thomas came closer, slicing the can just a bit on the side. The next shot went straight through the first can, sending it crashing backward into the woods with a loud crack.

Thomas grinned from ear to ear.

Uncle Tano slapped him on the back and laughed. "You're some shot, kid. Some shot!"

Thomas kept on shooting for a long time. He used up all the ammunition they carried, and even ran back for another box from the house.

Uncle Tano didn't seem to mind. Thomas could tell that the old man had known the pleasure of testing himself with a gun against a few rusty cans.

Chapter 7

That evening Tano filled the big pasta pot with water and put it on the stove to boil.

Thomas sat drawing by the window. He found himself working to recreate objects in and around Tano's cabin and spending less time on the elaborate "vacations" that filled the front of his notebook. Now, a tree or a rock or the big old-fashioned binoculars on the window ledge held his interest for hours. He even sketched a pretty good picture of Beauty snoozing on the couch. Uncle Tano propped it against a flowered tea cup on the mantel.

"A portrait of a beautiful lady!" he had said, smiling.

Thomas sat now, trying to capture on paper the carved wooden rocker that faced the window.

"I want to show you something," said Tano. "Come on." They went downstairs into the crowded cellar that was even cooler now and spookier in the dim light.

Tano pointed to the work table by the window. "You asked me about this," he said pointing.

Thomas saw the bits of glass and the tangle of metal ropes hanging above. He could see now that the ropes were flat on two sides and deeply grooved on the other two. They reminded Thomas of tiny railroad tracks.

"They're called 'cames,' " said Uncle Tano. They're made of lead. Let me show you." The old man bent down and rummaged through a dusty pile. He pulled out a large, flat package and laid it on the surface of the table. He carefully unwrapped the towel and rags, revealing a stained glass panel resting on a piece of plywood.

"It's the pond," said Thomas, impressed at his Uncle's skill.

Tano nodded. "I'm almost done with it," he said. He paused and rubbed the top of his bald head as if to show how hard the work had been.

"All the glass is in place, but the lead has to be soldered, so the whole thing stays together. I haven't worked on this thing for years, but it's been in my head to get it up, see the colors, get it done!"

"You've got good hands," he continued. "Like mine were . . . . Well . . . I thought you could help me finish this thing. It's been waiting for me for a long time." The old man looked at Thomas carefully. "Maybe it's been waiting for you."

Thomas smiled and followed the lead lines that outlined the shapes of glass. There was the pond, the island, even the two cedar trees, and the rowboat moored on the shore.

The shapes were blockier than the real thing, and some, like the water and the sky, were broken up. The lead line snaked its way around and through, connecting all the pieces like a big puzzle.

Another scene came into Thomas's mind . . . this one from long ago.

It was spring then, too, and the weather was warm. His father had come to visit and wanted to show Thomas some famous stained glass window in a church he had known as a boy. Thomas didn't want to go. "A church?" he had groaned. "Today?"

But his father had insisted.

The church was cool like the cellar. Thomas remembered the feel of his small hand held in his father's. As they stood before the window and looked up, Thomas's father began to talk. Thomas heard only "St. George," as the rest of his father's words became a droning sound, like background music.

Thomas had stared up at the picture before him. The bits of colored glass were painted with small details that enriched the scene. The glass, the paint, and the black lead line told an ancient story.

St. George was in full armour. His boyish face peered from the open helmet, topped by three plumes. In one hand, he carried a shield; in the other, a long pointed lance. His charging white horse leaped forward in an arc of muscle and courage. The body of the saint, the lance, and the horse all tensed at the same angle and pointed toward the enormous raging beast that loomed above them. The tip of the lance pierced the breast of the immense dragon, whose eyes flamed with fury and whose monstrous claws reached for the brave St. George, so tiny in comparison.

Against the dragon's amber-colored scales, glowed three drops of blood.

The sun had chosen that moment to shine with full force, igniting the colors of the glass and giving life to the figures. To Thomas, it seemed as if they waited each day for the warmth and the light to replay their deadly battle. He couldn't take his eyes off the scene. It felt familiar, somehow, and he longed to step into the picture to help the saint slay the scary beast.

Riding in the car back to Baltimore, his father had given Thomas a cherry lollipop that he sucked to a wafer thin circle. He remembered holding it up to the window and watching the sunlight set it aglow, blazing like the three drops of dragon blood in the church window.

It was the last time Thomas had seen his father.

Chapter 8

Thomas stood before the stained glass on the wooden worktable, his hands itching to hold the colored shards.

"Let me show you what we've got to do," said Tano, "and we'll start first thing in the morning. First, I need my glasses." He reached for a paint-splattered pair, its hinges wrapped with big wads of masking tape. "They still work!" he said, when he noticed Thomas staring.

Then the old man took out a jar and a paintbrush. "This is called 'flux,' " he said. "You brush this stuff on the lead, here, where the pieces meet—makes it easier for the solder to stick to the lead." He brushed a little on the joint, which held a piece of blue water glass next to the green glass of the shore.

He took out a soldering gun and plugged it into the socket. It looked a little like a real gun with a handle and a long tip.

"That tip gets very, very hot," said Tano, "so be careful!" After a few minutes, and with some difficulty, the old man held the soldering gun in one hand and a thick metal wire in the other. "This here," he said, pointing to the wire "is made from lead and tin. Watch." His hands shook as he touched the hot tip of the gun to the end of the wire. Thomas saw a drop of molten metal fall onto the seam where the lead wrapped around the glass, right where the flux had been painted. A few more drops were added for good measure.

"That should hold it," said Tano.

"Now you try. You've got the hands for it!"

The old man brushed the flux on a different joint. This one was the lead that held a side of the little white rowboat.

Thomas held the wire and the soldering gun, just as Tano did. He was terrified he'd make a mistake.

"Here, I'll help you," said the old man. He covered Thomas's right hand with his own gnarled one and guided the gun towards the wire. And though the skin was dry and wrinkled, Thomas could feel the old man's strength.

The wire melted and a drop hit the seam. "That's it," said Tano. "Now another. You do it. Good!" He touched the boy's shoulder, letting his hand rest there for a moment.

Thomas smiled.

He felt like he had anchored the little rowboat to the shore and now he wanted to do more.

"What next?" he asked, happily.

"No. Tomorrow," said Uncle Tano. "The water's probably boiling upstairs, and Beauty has to eat."

Thomas could hear the old cat yowling above them. He rolled his eyes and turned away from the work-table.

"Beauty! My beauty, my girl," called the old man as they climbed the stairs to the kitchen.

Tano fed the cat and began breaking spaghetti over the bubbling water. He stirred the strands with a big wooden fork and turned towards the salad.

"Here," he said, tearing the lettuce.

"Pour a little oil on this."

Thomas held the jar of thick green olive oil, letting a few generous drops slide over the leaves.

"Give me a little, too," said Tano, holding out his hands.

Thomas looked at him, dumbfounded.

"What?" he asked.

"Here, right on my hands," said the old man. "Just a little."

Thomas dribbled a puddle of oil onto Tano's upturned palms. The old man rubbed his hands together a few times. Then, as Thomas gaped, Tano wiped the whole slippery mess onto his nearly hairless head, scrubbing hard with his finger tips.

"Good for hair growth!" he said, looking up.

Thomas couldn't resist. "Looks like it's doin' a great job!" he said, laughing.

"Hey!" said Tano, shaking a fist at the boy. "I'm a tough guy. You better not make fun of me." But Thomas could see the old man was trying to keep a smile from erupting.

When dinner was done and their chocolate eaten, Thomas and Tano got ready for bed. Thomas brushed his teeth, changed into a T-shirt and hopped under the covers of his couch bed. He reached underneath for his sketchbook and pencil, while he watched Uncle Tano.

As usual, the old man barely changed from his day clothes. Thomas wondered if the old guy ever took a bath. His mother would kill him if he didn't take his nightly shower. It was kind of nice, he thought, not to be so careful, so squeaky clean all the time.

Tano removed his braided lather belt, hung it on the chair, bent to unlace his work boots and turned to click off the light. Beauty found her usual spot at the foot of the bed and closed her eyes. Something on the belt caught the last gleam from the light.

"What's that?" asked Thomas.

"What?" asked Tano. "What?"

"Something on your belt," said the boy, "something shining on your belt."

"Oh," said Tano, "it's nothing, go to sleep."

"Can I see it?" asked Thomas, dropping the pad and pencil and turning on the light. He glanced at the old man to check his mood, but Tano's face had that dreamy look, his eyes far away.

Thomas got out of bed and picked up the belt. Fastened on the inside was a gold ring. It had been cut to fit around one of the leather strips and hammered flat, so its shape lost the roundness of a finger. Now it was crushed into the braiding of the belt, a little slash of gold twinkling from the brown mesh, like buried treasure.

The old man watched the boy, and spoke slowly.

"Someone gave me that ring, almost 60 years ago," he said. "Her name was Clara . . . Clara. . . . She was little . . . skinny like a little bird . . . like a sparrow . . . like a beautiful sparrow. We were supposed to get married . . . she gave me the ring . . . but she was sick. She coughed and coughed . . . . She died a week before the wedding. Just a week! I couldn't keep her from dying. I couldn't protect my little sparrow! I couldn't keep her from suffering."

The old man wiped his eyes.

"Now," he said, "I have her ring . . . that's all. I put it on my belt, so she's always near me." He smiled sadly at Thomas and then his face stiffened. "And I vowed to myself, *never* will *I* suffer like that again! Never will I need anyone like that again! I made my place. I made it perfect. I don't need anything else! Now go to sleep!" he said sharply. "You can work on the panel tomorrow."

Thomas turned off the light. In the darkness he saw another ring . . . his mother's gold wedding ring. She had always worn it, and had a habit of twisting it whenever she was lost in thought.

One day he saw her crying by the phone. He knew his father had called. He saw her yank the ring off her finger and throw it against the wall. Thomas had followed the gleam of gold as it bounced and clicked to the floor, rolled a few feet, and landed by the kitchen door. He had picked it up, clutching it in his fist, and burning with anger. He wanted to hit his father, punish him for making his mother cry. But then, as always, he had pushed the anger down inside of himself. He was afraid that if he joined forces with his mother and shared in her anger, he might never see his father again. Thomas could tell she was giving up, so he had to hold on. He buried the ring deep under the socks in his top bureau drawer. It was there right now, a treasure he never wanted to find.

Chapter 9

Thomas woke to the sounds of someone crying. At first he thought it was his mother. Lately, she seemed to cry so easily that he began to link her image with the sound. But as his senses cleared, he realized that it was Uncle Tano, somewhere beyond the kitchen. He got out of bed quickly and quietly. He didn't know what to expect as he walked, barefoot, towards the sobs. He found the old man on the porch hunched over the body of Beauty, who lay on her side on the linoleum. Tano looked over his shoulder and wiped clumsily at his eyes. He didn't say a word. Thomas knelt down next to the old man and stroked the cat's fur. Her body had a strange hardness to it, unlike the feel of living flesh.

"What happened?" he asked quietly.

"She just died," said Tano. "She just died. Seventeen years old . . . old for a cat . . . old for anything! But she was lucky, you know. She went fast. I'm glad for her . . . my little Beauty." He picked up the stiff body and pressed it to his face.

One last sob escaped him and he stood up.

"I'm going to bury her," he said slowly. "I'll find a box and something to wrap her in."

Thomas felt helpless. What should he do? He hadn't really liked Beauty. And he couldn't help thinking how nice the house would smell without her. Then he felt ashamed. He knew how much she meant to Uncle Tano. He wandered into the living room and stood by the couch with its sheet and blanket thrown back. He glanced up at the mantel and saw the picture he had drawn: Beauty, sound asleep on the bed, her spindly tail curled around her.

Thomas, still barefoot, went down to the cellar. He wasn't sure what his plan was yet, but he had an idea. He brought along his drawing pencil. Uncle Tano rummaged noisily upstairs, looking for a box. Thomas had the cellar to himself. He found a piece of split wood, flat on one side and bark on the other, like a small version of the mantel over the fireplace. The flat side was smooth and light colored. Just right, he thought. After a moment, Thomas drew the first letter, lightly so he could change it if he made a mistake. He drew the second and third until it was finished. They curved in an arc at the top end of the wood: BEAUTY. Then, below the name, he drew a simple sketch of the old cat. He tried to capture her wide staring eyes and her crooked ears using only a few lines. *Okay*, he thought, *not bad*. Then he saw the soldering gun. Uncle Tano had shown him how to use it the night before, but he wasn't sure he could handle it properly. *Would it burn into the wood?* he wondered. *Could he try? And what if he broke it? The old man would have a fit, that was certain.*

Thomas picked up the soldering gun and plugged it in. Within minutes, the tip was hot. He touched the burning tip to the wood where the bottom of the *B* began. Slowly, carefully, he traced the letters. The burning wood smelled like a campfire, smoky, and rich, and satisfying. Each letter was deeply grooved into the wood, dark against light. Perfect! Next, he moved lower on the wood, to the face of the cat. He tried to stay on the pencil lines, but slipped on the curving line of the cheek. The tip of the gun made a brown slash, straight out from the face. *A whisker!* thought Thomas. He made two more just like it and three on the other side. Then, he burned in the eyes. Each was an almond shape with a straight line in the center running from top to bottom at the widest point. When he was done, Beauty stared out at Thomas just as she had that first night, with her cool cat eyes searching his.

He carried the wood upstairs where Uncle Tano had found the box that had held his work boots when they were brand new. Thomas wondered how long ago that was: one hundred years, maybe?

Now the old man was searching through a drawer, pulling out shirts frantically.

"Where is it?" he asked himself out loud. "Where is it?" Plaid shirts, flannel shirts, white dress shirts that Thomas couldn't picture Tano wearing, were scattered on the floor.

"Here it is," sighed the old man in relief. "This is the one." He pulled an ancient tissue-wrapped bundle from the bottom of the drawer. The tissue fell away and Tano held up an old-fashioned white shirt, badly yellowed along the sides and collar. "Silk," he said slowly "handmade . . . cost me a bundle. Had it made for my wedding . . . never wore it though," he said sadly. "This is the one."

Thomas and Tano went out to the porch. Beauty lay stiff and still on the floor. Gently, Tano wrapped her in the old silk shirt, covering her head and tail. Then he put her into the box and closed the lid.

"We've got to dig a grave," he said. "Let's get the shovels."

Thomas followed the old man downstairs.

"Smells smoky down here," said Tano sniffing the air. Thomas didn't say a word. He wanted to surprise Uncle Tano when the grave was finished.

Tano rowed to the little island in the middle of the pond. Thomas held the wooden marker on his lap, covered by the big square box that held Beauty.

They dug a hole between the two cedars and covered Beauty with the dirt. Just as they finished, Thomas went back to the boat and brought over the grave marker. He handed it to Uncle Tano. The old man was shocked. He looked at the arc of letters burned into the wood and saw they way they floated protectively over the face of the cat. He grabbed the boy roughly and hugged him close.

Thomas could feel the old man's body shake. Tano straightened up, pulled a much-used handkerchief from his back pocket, and loudly blew his nose. Then he planted the marker directly over the spot where Beauty lay buried. He made sure that the front of the marker faced the house, so it could be seen from the picture window.

Thomas rowed back to shore while Uncle Tano muttered. "That's it! Never again! No more pets!"

Chapter 10

The next morning, Thomas was up before the old man. He was anxious to work on the leaded glass panel in the cellar.

"Can I use the soldering gun today?" he asked.

"I don't know why not," said Tano, smiling. "Looks to me like you're already an expert with that thing."

They spent the morning soldering each seam on the bottom section of the panel, taking care to put just enough solder, but not too much. Uncle Tano didn't want lumps on his picture of the pond.

They stopped for lunch, then went back downstairs to work.

Thomas could see that Uncle Tano's hands were shaky, and he had trouble seeing the thin line of the joint. Thomas did more and more of the soldering. He was happy doing this and he knew he was good at it.

"I'm going up," said the old man, "be by myself for a while . . . just sit quietly for a few minutes." He sadly climbed the cellar stairs, as Thomas watched. Then the boy turned back to his work and he was happy again.

This time when his mother called, his voice was different. He told her that Beauty had died and how they had buried her on the island. Then he described the stained glass panel. "I got to use the soldering gun!" he said. "It's fun!"

"Sounds like a lot has happened down there!" said his mother. "How's Uncle Tano?"

"Okay," answered Thomas. "He's right here."

His mother and Tano talked for a while as Thomas set the table for dinner.

Probably the same old stuff again, thought Thomas, as he placed the glasses and forks. Tano hung up and ladled out their food.

Sure enough, Thomas looked down at a large bowl of spaghetti.

This time, instead of tomato sauce or broccoli, there were peas. Thomas's face must have shown some disgust because Tano said, "What's the matter? You like spaghetti, don't you?"

"Yeah," said Thomas. "But not every day!"

"It's good for you!" Tano said, breaking off a piece of bread.

"Don't you eat anything else?" asked the boy.

"Sure I do," said Tano. "I make macaroni, sometimes, and ravioli, too! But those are for special occasions."

"That's all the same," said Thomas. "What about chicken or fish or hamburgers or pizza?"

"Pizza? I suppose I could make pizza," said Tano, doing his regular routine with the wadded up bread.

"Make pizza?" asked Thomas.

"Sure. I've done it a few times: bread dough, sauce, a little cheese. Okay, tomorrow we make pizza!"

Thomas rolled his eyes. He had been hoping to eat the kind of pizza that came in a big white box.

Chapter 11

The morning was cool and gray. Mist hung over the pond, shrouding the little island.

"Smells like rain," said Tano. "Good day to work on the panel—finish it up and hang it."

The soldering gun was plugged in after breakfast and work began. Thomas was pleased with the way he handled the gun and the melting metal. He knew exactly how long to hold the wire to the tip of the gun, and how many drops to allow to fall. He couldn't wait to see the panel finished, hanging in the sun.

"You're getting good at this," said Tano. "I think I'll go up and start that pizza dough."

Thomas worked on in silence as the first few raindrops splattered against the window.

Loud, harsh honks filled the air over the house and Thomas jumped. The sounds got louder and louder and Thomas looked out to see a flock of five, heavy-bodied Canada geese descending on the pond, squawking and gobbling as they splash-landed into the water.

He heard Tano shouting above him.

"Damn geese! They'll take over. They'll ruin my pond!" And then, "Not this year!"

The screen door slapped loudly and Thomas saw Uncle Tano running with the rifle. The boy jumped up, burned his hand on the tip of the soldering gun, and yanked it out of the socket. He ran up the stairs and out the back door to the sounds of gunshots.

Thomas screamed, "No!"

But Tano fired again. "I'm only trying to scare them!" shouted the old man. "I don't want to kill them!" But his voice was drowned by the sounds of the terrified geese. They were flying in all directions, wings flapping, honking wildly.

Trying to stop the noise and confusion, Thomas grabbed the old man's arm just as another shot was fired. He heard a different kind of honk, a cry, in the split second after the rifle's crack. Then he saw a goose drop heavily from the squawking flock. It splashed into the water, righted itself, and struggled madly to lift off.

Thomas and Tano stood horrified.

"Damnation!" shouted the old man. "What the hell were you doing? I was only trying to scare them away!"

"I thought you were going to kill them!" Thomas cried. "I didn't mean to. . . ."

They were watching the poor goose beating at the water. It lifted off and they could see its bloody leg, dangling uselessly. Again, it fell back into the pond.

"Well, now I *really* have to kill it!" screamed Tano, red-faced and furious.

"No!" shouted Thomas. "No! You can't!"

"Yes, I can!" yelled Tano. "It's only going to suffer. You know that!" The old man spit out the words, and aimed the gun at the floundering bird.

"No!" cried Thomas. "I won't let you!" He grabbed at the rifle, and pulled as hard as he could. Uncle Tano lost his balance and came crashing on top of him as he fell backward in the wet grass.

The old man sat up. The rifle lay beside him. Thomas was crying, tears and rain mixing on his face.

"Please," he begged. "Please don't kill him. Just because he's not perfect, just because he's wounded. We can fix him. We can try. Please, please!" he sobbed, "We can try!"

The old man looked at the boy and then at the goose. It was trying to gain momentum. Its neck stretched taut with the effort, but its strength was giving out. Clouds of dark blood billowed in the water around it.

"Damnation!" Tano shouted to the whole world. "Damnation!"

It was raining heavily now, and Thomas slipped as he tried getting up.

"We've got to catch him," said Tano. "Then we can call the vet. Let her handle this."

He ran to the cellar and brought out a large piece of canvas, a ground cloth he used to cover the plants when he painted the outside of the house. It was big and strong enough for wrapping a goose.

Thomas watched the goose struggling. He could see that it was moving more slowly now.

"You get in the boat," Tano said to Thomas, "and row toward the goose. Try to get him on the land."

Thomas waded into the pond and jumped in the rowboat. His sneakers sloshed in the rainwater collecting in the bottom. He rowed as fast as he could, aiming at the goose with the tip of the boat, pushing it towards shore. But the goose veered sharply to the right, swimming in a lopsided panic, frantic to fly but exhausted and bleeding badly.

"Use the oars!" shouted Tano, holding the canvas like a bullfighter's cape, running in the rain.

"Scare him toward that bank," he said, pointing to the curve by the rocks. "I'll come around the back."

Again, Thomas rowed toward the goose, but stopped about ten feet away. While the boat drifted forward, he lifted the oars—one on the left, one on the right—pointing them at the goose like arrows. He waved the heavy oars as best he could so the goose, sensing the danger on either side, pushed through the water in a straight line toward shore.

Thomas kept it up and the rowboat inched forward. The goose took one last flight, only a foot above the water, and landed heavily on the wet grass.

Tano waited behind the rocks and pounced, throwing himself and the canvas over the large bird.

"Hurry!" screamed the old man. "Help me!" Thomas reached the shore and ran to the thrashing bundled that squawked and screeched under Uncle Tano. The goose's head popped out. Its beak snapped and hissed.

"Watch out! He'll bite you!" yelled the old man, leaning all his weight on the goose.

Thomas ripped off his flannel shirt and threw it over the goose's head. Tano grabbed the sleeve and together they had the goose pretty well wrapped, though one dark foot hung from the canvas.

"Gotta get to the car," grunted Tano.

"Careful! Watch the beak!"

Slowly, they inched around the side of the pond. Rain streamed down their faces and the mud sucked at their shoes. The goose's body was heavy under the canvas covering. It was struggling less now, though it still tried to fling off the flannel hood. Thomas's hand was under its chest. Through the heavy fabric, he could feel the rapid beat of the bird's heart.

Trying to keep their balance on the slippery hill, Thomas and Tano stumbled toward the car.

"The keys!" shouted Tano as if he just realized they were necessary to start the car. "On the table . . . by the phone!"

The old man got a better grip on the bird, but didn't look too secure.

"Hurry!" he yelled.

Thomas ran into the house and grabbed the keys. He lurched out the door and ran down to the car where Uncle Tano was about to drop the goose, the canvas, and himself onto the soggy grass.

"The trunk! Open the trunk!" coughed the old man.

Thomas fumbled for a second. "Which key?" Then he stuck one in, opened the trunk, and turned to help Tano lower the big bird into the cavity. It was littered with rags and old National Geographic magazines.

"I always meant to take them to the dump," said the old man, as they slammed the lid on the hissing goose. "Go get another shirt!" he yelled at Thomas.

The ride was short and silent. Tano concentrated on the road ahead, all anger and intensity. Thomas sat motionless, afraid that the goose wouldn't survive the trip in the trunk.

Chapter 12

The vet came out to the car when she heard what they had brought. Her name was Dr. Cole and she donned heavy work gloves as she walked.

Tano opened the trunk and revealed the goose, who had managed to wriggle out of the canvas wrapping and now tried to stand. Thomas saw the blood soaked leg and the stain on the floor of the trunk.

"He'll live, won't he?" asked Thomas.

"We'll see," said Dr. Cole. "I'll take her inside and check her out. That leg looks pretty bad."

"Her?" asked Thomas. "It's a her?"

"I think so," said the vet. But I won't know for sure until I examine her. Male and female geese look alike. I just have a feeling, though. Here, help me carry her to the office."

The hissing goose was wrapped in the canvas once more. Dr. Cole held the head, clamping down securely on the beak. She and Thomas managed to get the goose past the staring dog and cat owners who shared the waiting room with their pets. A big, black mutt jumped and barked when he caught the scent of the bundle they carried.

"Here," said Dr. Cole. "Lay her on the floor and I'll get to work. You'll have to wait outside for a while."

She called her assistant and disappeared behind the office door.

Tano and Thomas sat with the others.

A woman with a trembling Chihuahua asked what everyone wanted to know.

"What happened to the goose? Hit it with your car, did you?"

Uncle Tano had little patience for most people and he was not happy to be here.

"No!" he said abruptly.

"Well, what did you do? Find it like that, bloody and all?"

"No!" said Tano more sharply than before.

"We shot her by accident," said Thomas. "Dr. Cole is going to fix her up."

"Oh," said another woman, trying to talk over her yelping Dalmatian. "That's terrible. Those birds mate for life, you know."

Like people, thought Thomas. Like people *should* anyway.

Thomas looked at Tano. He knew the old man was thinking he should have put it out of its misery. A bloody leg and a lost mate, more suffering. . . .

"Damn!" said Tano, looking at the floor.

She's got to be all right, Thomas thought. *She's got to be all right and get back to her mate*. He closed his eyes and wished that, for once, it would end up okay.

After a long, long time, Dr. Cole appeared and apologized to all the people in the waiting room. Some had given up and gone home.

"As you know," she said, "we've had an emergency. I'll be back in a minute." She looked at Uncle Tano and Thomas and ushered them into her back office.

"The goose is a bit shaky," said Dr. Cole, "but I think she'll make it. I had to amputate the leg. The bullet tore into the large bone and there was no way to save it. She'll have to stay here for a few days, and then, if she's okay, you can bring her home. Will she live at your place?" she asked the old man.

"What? My place? I can't have a goose there! Wreck my pond . . . poop all over . . . it's a wild thing . . . not a pet . . . I can't have a goose!"

"Well. I can call the state people," said the vet. "They might take it. . . . Or Audubon. But I know they're pretty full during this season. Spring, you know. Babies of every sort—birds that have fallen from nests, orphaned fawns, injured woodchucks."

"Enough!" said Tano. "I get the picture."

"I'll try," said Dr. Cole. "Let's wait and see. I don't know how she'll do . . . but, she might make it. If she can hop on one leg, it shouldn't interfere with feeding or swimming. . . . As long as she can fly, she might be all right. She's lucky it wasn't the wing. We'll just have to see. Anyway, call me tomorrow and I'll let you know how she's doing."

"I don't want to know," said Tano.

"I do," said Thomas. "I want to know."

Tano looked at the boy and rolled his eyes.

"Get in the car," he said.

Still soaked to the skin, they drove silently back to

the house. The rain had not let up, making the ride slower than usual.

As he drove, Tano mumbled, his eyes angrily fixed on the road. "Should have shot the bird right there at the pond," he said. "Finished . . . over . . . no more suffering. . . . And," he said bitterly, "no expense on top of everything!"

Thomas watched the windshield wipers swish back and forth and wondered what to name a Canada goose with one leg.

Chapter 13

Thomas called his mother that night and Dr. Cole the next afternoon, as promised. Tano pretended not to care, but he stood close enough to hear the boy's end of the conversation.

"She couldn't find a place for the goose, and hopes we can take her here," Thomas said happily. "Dr. Cole has a kennel out back and she can keep her there for a while, but she's afraid the dogs will drive her crazy. It's not good for the 'healing process'," said Thomas, quoting Dr. Cole's words.

"Damn!," said Tano, turning away from the boy. "Let me think . . . tell her I'll call her back."

Thomas was crushed. He mumbled Tano's instructions to Dr. Cole and hung up.

"What's gonna happen to her if we don't take her?" he cried. "We're responsible for her!"

"Responsible? Responsible?" Uncle Tano's face had tightened into an angry mask as he shouted.

"No one is responsible in this whole damn world! People do stupid, selfish things! Look at my life! A kid thrown here and there. . . . They shouldn't have had me if they couldn't take care of me . . . and you. Look at your father! Responsible? He left his wife and kid . . . for what? For nothing! . . . just because he couldn't be responsible!"

Thomas was pale. His eyes widened and his whole body began to shake.

Uncle Tano kept it up. "We should have shot the damn goose when we had the chance!"

Thomas threw himself at the old man, beating at him with his fists.

"Take that back!" he screamed. "Take that back! My father didn't leave us . . . he didn't!"

Tano held the boy's arms, shocked by the power of his own words.

"I hate you!" sobbed Thomas. "I hate you. . . . I hate you. . . . I hate him!"

The old man heard Thomas's last words and pulled the boy to him. Thomas wept long and hard: a flood that poured from years of pent up anger and a deep well of sadness.

Then Tano said something he hadn't said in a long, long time. He said it quietly and stroked the boy's hair.

"I'm sorry, kid; I really am."

Thomas looked up and wiped his face. He was relieved. He had said it. He did hate his father. He loved him, too, but he knew deep down that the disappointment he felt was real. Thomas could hate him for leaving; his father deserved it.

A picture of a little boy flashed in Thomas's mind: a little boy on a big ship . . . a scared, disappointed, angry little boy with a face like his own. In that instant, the link between himself and his great uncle was clear. It felt as solid and real as the chain that held the little rowboat to its mooring by the pond.

Uncle Tano held Thomas by the shoulders and looked straight into the boy's eyes. It was a different stare than on that first day. Thomas felt an acceptance, a look that spoke of understanding and even friendship.

"You're right about the goose," said Tano. "We didn't shoot it. We saved it. So now we are responsible . . . no one else . . . us."

"She'll come here?" asked Thomas brightly.

"She'll come here," said the old man, throwing up his hands. "What the hell else can we do?"

Thomas lunged forward and hugged Uncle Tano and the old man hugged him back.

Uncle Tano eyed the door to the cellar. His face brightened. "Let's finish the damn panel before that damn goose arrives!" he said. "Who knows what the hell will happen then!"

Thomas was ecstatic. He held the soldering gun and the wire and moved expertly over the surface of the stained glass. His hands moved as if they had a life of their own: Flux, melt, drip . . . flux, melt, drip.

Uncle Tano turned on an old radio and found a station playing opera. Thomas hated opera with its screeching high notes and quivering voices. But he found himself smiling when the old man started to sing along, mixing up the words badly. Tonight they were having pizza in a white box, picked up on the way back from the vet. Last night's efforts had been a disaster. They had returned to find the pizza dough risen past the edges of the bowl, dripping onto the table and floor. He and the old man had eaten cereal for dinner. But tonight—"real" pizza and the homecoming of the goose to look forward to in a few days. He had lots of stories to tell his mother, too, but all of that was in the future. Here, now, in this damp cellar, working with his hands and listening to the swelling chords mix with the sound of the rain, Thomas felt content. He was surprised by this, but he didn't stop to think about it. His hands moved, and his eyes saw, and his ears listened, and the pieces fit together like a big puzzle.

Chapter 14

Thomas heard it in his dreams. *Ka-ronk! Ka-ronk! Ka-ronk!*

The goose flew and squawked, circling above him in a cloudless sky.

But then he was awake, eyes open, and staring up at the shadows on the living room ceiling. The harsh ka-ronking continued.

Thomas went to the window and saw a single goose hunched on the island, right over Beauty's grave! In the moonlight, he could just make out the flash of white on its cheeks as the dark head pointed toward the sky. "*Ka-ronk . . . ka-ronk*," it called, over and over. *Was it the goose's mate?* he wondered. *Was he waiting for her to return? And how long*, he thought, *will he wait?* Thomas closed his eyes and sent a silent message to the lonely goose: *If you are* our goose's *mate*, he thought, please, *please wait for her.* Wait until she comes back from Dr. Cole's. Please wait!

He crept back to his bed and tried to think of a way to keep the goose on the pond. *We could feed it*, he thought. Then he pictured Uncle Tano's face as he told him of the plan. "I'll think of something," he whispered. "I have to."

He tried to put himself to sleep in his usual way, but a family vacation just didn't appear. He hadn't done this for several nights. When he thought about it, he was surprised, for he hadn't missed his imaginary travels at all. Until tonight, he hadn't noticed that he had stopped. He was more interested in his daytime sketchbook, his target practice, the stained glass, and now, in what would happen to the geese. He could hear low ka-ronks coming from the island. Would the goose wait long enough? Would the injured goose be able to live on the pond?

Just as he drifted off to sleep, Thomas had a strange and troubling thought. What if Uncle Tano had been right? What if it was more cruel to have saved the goose than to have finished her off?

He remembered the starling which Beauty had caught on his first day here. He would have put it in a box and kept it safe until it died. Was that more cruel than Tano's swift chop of the hatchet? Would the starling have suffered more if Thomas had been allowed to "nurse" it? Would he be doing it for himself or for the bird? And what of the muskrat babies? Would they have suffered a horrible, painful death if Tano hadn't killed them quickly with the rifle? He had no answer to these questions. He wished there was one rule that you could follow . . . something to tell you when to hold on and when to end it.

His thoughts turned to the one-legged goose. It was too late now to wonder what should have been done. Like Uncle Tano said, she was their responsibility and they had to take it. She was counting on them and Thomas knew he wouldn't let her down. She was coming here and she was his responsibility, as much, if not more than Uncle Tano's. *Whatever happens*, he thought, *this is a time to hold on.*

The next morning, Thomas leaped out of bed and went straight to the window. The goose on the island was still there, sleeping with its head buried under its huge wing.

"Look!" said Thomas, pointing to the bird. Uncle Tano had just gotten up and came stumbling to the window next to the boy.

"It's her mate," said Thomas. "I know it!"

"Oh you know it, do you?" asked the old man. "Well, you're probably right. The others are too frightened to come back now."

"I was thinking . . .," said Thomas at breakfast. He spoke slowly, watching Tano's expression. "I was thinking that . . . that maybe we could feed the goose and keep him here. So our goose will have a family when she gets back."

"Oh, great!" said Tano. "Feed the goose! We'll have every damn animal coming here for a free meal! We'll never get rid of them! Thomas," he said slowly, "Let the goose be. We've already meddled too much as it is."

The goose stayed all that day, swimming on the pond and feeding on the banks. When Thomas wasn't outside, he found himself running to the window to check on the goose. He was afraid the bird might fly away every time he turned his back.

By lunchtime, Tano was losing patience with the boy.

"Why don't you just go down there and live with the damn goose? You can't take your eyes off him!"

Thomas smiled and picked up his sketchbook. "Mind if I take my lunch outside?" he asked.

The old man kept eating his bread and cheese. He waved his hand, as if to say, "Go ahead, I don't care."

Thomas walked in a wide circle around the pond. He certainly didn't want to scare the goose away. He found the flat rock that they had used for target practice and sat down.

The goose was sitting on the shore watching Thomas watching him. His head was turned and alert to any movement.

He's *beautiful*, thought Thomas. *Handsome, really.* He wished he could stroke the goose's tawny brown back and long, black neck.

Thomas especially liked the white patch that wrapped around the goose's chin and went up the cheeks almost to the top of his head. It gave him the look of someone wrapped in a white bandage, like those old-fashioned pictures of patients with terrible toothaches. The white patch framed his head drawing attention to his bright eyes—eyes that looked like black jelly beans or shiny olives. *Yes, he is handsome*, thought Thomas. *A handsome male for our one-legged goose.*

"I guess I've got two geese to name now," he said to himself.

As Thomas watched, he began to draw. He sketched in the heavy body and outlined the graceful neck. He tried to capture the way the eye sat in the head and how the beak curved gently downward. Again and again he erased the lines until the white paper was a blur of gray smudges.

He heard the screen door slam on the back porch and wondered where Uncle Tano was going. Then he heard the squish of the big work boots in the muddy grass behind him. He was instantly aware of all the goose poop on the grass and the scattered wing feathers littering the lawn. He braced himself for some shouting, but instead the old man said quietly:

"Here, let me try." Uncle Tano looked at the goose sitting ahead of them. He crouched beside Thomas's rock and began a rough sketch of the head and neck of the goose. Even though the old man's hands looked gnarly and coarse, the line he drew was as delicate as any Thomas had ever seen. "That's really good!" said Thomas. "Can you teach me?"

"You're already pretty good," said Uncle Tano. "Just need a little fine tuning."

"Always check out the distances," he said. "Like the neck to the body, the eye to the head. If it looks wrong go back to the source. Look at the goose. . . . See those connections? See those points?"

Thomas did. He tried again and though his goose head wasn't perfect, it was better than the last one.

They sat on the rock for a long time. Some of the drawings were terrible. "Don't worry about it," said Uncle Tano. "Try again. See . . . look again . . . over and over . . . can't help but get better."

The old man got up and stretched. The goose did

the same. He stood, spread his wings and waddled slowly to the pond, his heavy body swaying from side to side like a paunchy old gunslinger heading down Main Street.

Thomas laughed and looked at Tano.

"Doc! Doc Holiday or maybe Wyatt! Wyatt Earp? No, Doc . . . Doc!"

"What the hell are you saying?" asked Tano, certain the boy had gone mad.

"Doc! That's his name. Doc! The gunslinger from the OK Corral. . . . That's what we'll call the goose!"

"We won't call him anything," said Tano. "You will!"

The old man walked away muttering about the goose poop.

The goose swam peacefully, unaware of his new name. Thomas turned back to watch him and began a new drawing. He sketched in the feathers and let the rich black of his ebony pencil color the goose's beautiful neck. The white paper became the cheek patch. At the bottom of the page, in light short strokes, he sketched in the texture of the water.

Thomas looked at his drawing and smiled. He felt calmer, closer, more connected to the bird in some way, as if he'd made a rope to hold the goose and keep it at the pond.

He gathered his things and marched up to the house.

"Pretty damn good," said Tano holding the sketchbook. "Pretty damn good!"

Chapter 15

"So what should we name her?" asked Thomas.

It was a bright, cool morning, just the right morning, he thought for picking up an injured goose. Thomas had gotten up very early to check on Doc. He was thrilled to see the beautiful male sunning himself on the dew-covered lawn.

"Name her?" said Tano. "That's your department, not mine."

I was thinking of Lavinia," said Thomas, watching the old man for a reaction. "Or Penelope!" He knew this was going to be a rough morning and that Uncle Tano would complain. But he had gotten to know the old man pretty well by now and he no longer thought of him as a volcano. Grumpy and unpredictable for sure, but definitely not dangerous. Thomas went on bravely with his teasing.

"Or Gertrude. What about Gertrude?"

"Be quiet!" said Tano. "And get in the car. We've got to do some shopping on the way, so get moving! Hey!" he shouted, as Thomas went to open the passenger door, "don't forget the canvas. That damn goose will bite you again if you're not careful. She's not going to be grateful for all this, I can tell you."

Chapter 16

Before going to the vet's, Tano and Thomas headed for the local STOP & SHOP. They wandered the aisles, picking up provisions for the rest of the week.

"What kind of cereal do you want?" asked the old man. "Not that candy-colored crap, I hope."

Thomas smiled. "No," he answered. "The crap we've been eating is just fine!"

"Watch out, young man!" said Tano glaring. Then, without thinking, he grabbed a can of Friskies cat food from the shelf and tossed it in the cart.

The old man looked at Thomas. His eyes looked softened and sad when he realized his mistake.

"She loved this kind," he said reading the label: "Mixed Grill." "What the hell do they mix in that grill? You'll never know! They should say exactly what's in there," he said. "Pig's snouts, cow's ears, turkey eyeballs! What's wrong with that?" Tano's voice got louder as he spoke and some of the other customers were beginning to stare. "What's wrong with that?" he repeated, placing the can back on the shelf.

Leading his uncle, Thomas pushed the cart swiftly to the fresh produce section and stopped in front of the fruits.

Tano picked up a peach and sniffed it dramatically, his nose flat up against the fuzzy skin. He did this to several others and moved on to the plums.

"It's gotta have that smell," he told Thomas. "That real *fruity* smell."

Thomas, afraid the nearby shoppers would notice the old man's unusual way of choosing fruit, and even more concerned that Uncle Tano might take a bite or two in search of the "real fruity taste," rushed quickly to the vegetables. He loaded the cart with broccoli, zucchini, and lettuce, knowing that Tano liked them all.

By the time they arrived at the checkout counter, Thomas was exhausted. It was one thing to deal with the old man's nuttiness by himself, and another to do it in public!

"Have a nice day!" chirped the smiling cashier.

"Yeah, yeah," said Tano grumpily.

Thomas rolled his eyes as they headed toward the car.

Chapter 17

The old man was right about the goose not being grateful. When Dr. Cole brought her out, wrapped in a blanket, the big bird was as snippy and hissy as ever. She was probably scared out of her wits and struck at anything that came close.

They all walked carefully to the car while Dr. Cole talked.

"I've put in the kind of stitches that dissolve," she said. "Give her some time and she should be totally healed. She's been hopping around pretty well here, so I think she'll be OK."

"And her mate is waiting for her!" said Thomas beaming.

"Oh!" said Dr. Cole. "The gander stayed around? Great!"

"Yeah, great!" said Tano. "Let's get moving." They put the goose in the trunk for the short ride back to the house.

"Thanks!" yelled Thomas from the front seat.

"Call me if you need help!" shouted the vet, as she waved good-bye.

"Help?" muttered Tano. "We'll need help, believe me!"

They managed to get the goose out of the trunk, with just a few nasty nips on the hands. She headed

straight for the water, in short, powerful hops, ka-
ronking all the way.

Thomas stood on the bank, barely breathing, aware
of the wild thumping in his chest. He watched the
scene unfold, as if in slow motion . . . a strange ballet
of two geese on a little patch of water.

It was one of those moments when all other sound
and movement seemed to disappear—as if the whole
world had stopped to watch the homecoming.

The gander floated quietly and pointed his sleek,
dark head at the creature hopping awkwardly toward
him. He was silent, watchful, confused by the unfa-
miliar movements.

With all his being, Thomas willed the goose to stay.

"Don't go!" he whispered. . . . "Please don't fly
away!"

The female hit the water and headed gracefully toward the male. He remained motionless, still wary. And then there was a small angling of his head. He recognized her! He knew her! He swam to meet her and began to call. They met near the island, bumped up against each other and began honking happily.

Soon the pond echoed with the loud, joyful greetings of the two birds.

Thomas looked up at the old man and saw him smiling.

That afternoon Thomas sat on the wide flat rock watching the two geese intently. He drew and watched for a long time in the spring air. He could smell the grass and see the turtles sunning themselves on the warm rocks. He tried to remember uncle Tano's advice from yesterday: Look at the source, check the distances. The drawings got better and better.

Thomas watched as the geese swam, turning and gliding in unison. Alone, each goose was beautiful, he thought; but together, they were magnificent. He finished a drawing of the couple, one following the other, with their sleek, black necks and their happy, jelly bean eyes.

Tano emerged from the cellar.

"Come here!" he shouted to Thomas.

"Come here!"

Thomas grabbed his sketchbook and ran to the cellar door.

Uncle Tano had edged the glass panel in polished

pine with two wire loops on top so he could hang it from the frame of the picture window.

"Let's put it up," said the old man.

Upstairs, Tano measured the distance for the wire loops. He hammered two nails into the top of the frame on the left side of the window. Then holding the panel in two hands, he lifted it up, trying to loop the wires on the nails.

"I can't get that one," he grunted.

Thomas climbed up on the wide ledge under the window. His body filled the height of the picture window and he felt he could fly out into the sunshine.

"Here. Over here," said Tano, still holding the heavy panel.

Thomas stretched up and secured the loop on the nail.

Tano stood back.

"Look!" he said, his face beaming, "look what we made!" He held his hand out to Thomas and helped the boy down.

The sunlight blazed through the colors: the deep greens of the tree shapes, the lighter greens of the grass, the pale blue sky with its milky white clouds, and the swirly turquoise glass of the pond.

How strange it looked to Thomas. Their perfect stained glass picture, glowing with light, set inside the larger, real picture outside the window. The real pond, and grass, and trees—not perfect but also glowing and growing and humming with life. He didn't know which was more beautiful. And then they heard the familiar ka-ronking of the geese. Thomas and Tano looked out to see the birds splashing water over their heads and thrusting their beaks deep into the muddy pools by the banks.

"That's what's missing from the picture," said Thomas, smiling. "The geese!"

"Aah!" said the old man. But he stopped himself. It was done. The geese were here to stay.

Chapter 18

Thomas put himself to sleep that night with a list of names. Fannie, Bess, Myrtle—he had to name the goose before he went home. He only had one more night before his mother would come on Sunday morning. It was funny, he thought as his eyes closed; it seemed like he'd been here forever.

During the night, he heard the harsh squawks of the geese mixed with softer mutterings. As before, he hopped quickly out of bed and went to the window. At first he could only see the shadow of one goose and he feared that Doc had taken off, leaving his one-legged mate behind. But then he made out another shape, sitting on the island near one of the cedar trees.

Thomas had seen the geese there while he drew that afternoon, sometimes with a stick or twig in their beaks.

It came to him. "A nest!" he whispered. "They've got a nest!"

He turned to get back under the covers and saw Uncle Tano's belt. There was just enough light to pick out the gold ring, as on the night he'd heard the old man's story.

"Clara!" he said out loud. "Clara!"

"Wha . . . ?" asked Tano drowsily. His head lifted from the pillow. "What's wrong?"

"Nothing," said Thomas. "I've got a name for the goose! Clara," he said, smiling.

Uncle Tano's eyes narrowed and he stared furiously at the boy. Thomas could only make out their angry gleam. He waited. And then he saw the dark shape of the old man's head fall back on the pillow. "All right," he heard from the shadows and then again, this time sighing heavily, "all right. . . . Now go to sleep!"

"They're making a nest!" whispered Thomas in the dark.

"I know," said Tano softly, "I know."

Chapter 19

It was Thomas's last day. Uncle Tano was unusually quiet, bustling around in the kitchen.

After breakfast, the old man suggested a walk to the ocean.

"We haven't been off this damn property for two weeks!" he said.

"I'd rather stay here and draw," said Thomas.

"Suit yourself," said Tano, "but there's a job I'd like you to help me with."

Later, they sat on the linoleum floor of the screened porch and removed the cat door that Beauty had used for so many years. The door was tufted with gray-brown fur, caught in the comings and goings of the ancient cat. Thomas looked at the old man but Tano kept busy: he measured the door quickly and cut a rough piece of wood to fill the space. Thomas held the wood while Tano nailed it shut forever.

Beauty was gone. The geese were here. Uncle Tano had let them stay, even though they'd mess up his "perfect place."

It wasn't easy, thought Thomas, but the old man had changed since that first day two long weeks ago. It was a little change, but a good change. *Maybe*, thought Thomas, *maybe I've changed a little, too.*

"All right," said Tano sadly, "we're done now. You can go."

Thomas ran towards the pond with his sketchbook and pencil. The geese were aware of his presence, but unafraid.

He started drawing the geese, but soon was filling page after page with sketches of the pond, the rocks, even the little house on the hill.

There were only a few blank pages left in his sketchbook when he stopped drawing.

Uncle Tano greeted him at the top of the stone stairs that led to the terrace.

"Let's eat out here tonight," he said. "The weather's warm enough and look at the sky." They both looked up. "Beautiful, isn't it?"

Thomas was relieved that the old man was in a good mood.

"Sounds great," he said. "We're having the usual?"

"If you mean spaghetti," said the old man, "no, we're not. While you were out drawing, I made us some real old-fashioned Sicilian pizza! It's in the oven."

Thomas was wide-eyed. He could smell the pizza and it made him instantly hungry.

They ate out on the terrace, under the gazebo. The setting sun streaked the sky with gold. It lit the trees and reflected in the ripples of the pond water. *It's peaceful here*, thought Thomas. *Peaceful and beautiful and now, with the geese, full of life.*

Uncle Tano drank his wine and stared out at the little island with the wooden marker.

"When will the baby geese be born?" asked Thomas.

"Goslings," said the old man. "Oh, in a month or so. The place will be a mess then!" he smiled.

"But I've got to go home tomorrow!" said Thomas. "I don't want to go yet!" he almost shouted, shocked to recognize his own feelings.

Uncle Tano looked at Thomas. His blue eyes weren't quite as sharp as they had been, and now they filled with tears.

Softly he said, "You can come back, you know. Come back this summer. The goslings will be here . . . Clara will be here . . ." His voice trailed off.

Thomas's own eyes reddened. "I'd like that," he said quietly.

As the two got ready for bed, Tano spoke.

"Well," he said, taking off his work boots, "tomorrow, after you go, I'll take a nice bath. Maybe shave, too. Nah . . . I don't want to overdo it. A bath is plenty. Lasts a few weeks."

Thomas smiled and shook his head.

"What's the matter? Laughing at me?" asked the old man.

"No, no!" answered Thomas. "I was thinking of something else."

"Oh, sure," said Tano. "I know you think I'm a little cuckoo." He twirled his finger by the side of his head. "But I do all right . . . I do all right. . . . *We* did all right these last two weeks, too."

"Yeah," said Thomas. "We did."

Chapter 20

Thomas's mother arrived right after lunch. She yoo-hooed into the screen door but got no answer. When she came around to the other side of the house, she looked down at the pond. There, on a flat rock on the far bank, sat Thomas and Uncle Tano watching the two geese as they fussed over their crude nest by the cedar tree.

"Hi, guys!" she yelled across the water. Neither Thomas nor Tano looked up, so she climbed down the hill and waved at them as she walked.

Thomas noticed and ran toward her. They crashed together and nearly fell over, laughing and hugging.

"You look taller, Hon, you really do! And you look filthy! Have you had a bath recently?"

"Ma," said Thomas, "look what they're doing!" He pulled her along by the hand and stopped at the flat rock where Tano sat smiling.

"You've had some two weeks!" she said to her uncle, kissing him on the cheek.

"How's my sister doing?" he asked.

"She'll be around for a while," said Thomas's mother, putting her arm around her son. "Like the rest of us, she's a pretty tough bird!"

She smiled and turned toward Thomas.

"Sweetie pie, we've got to get moving. We've got a long ride, and I *know* I'll be doing a lot of laundry when I get home!"

"First, look at Clara and Doc," said Thomas directing his mother back to the island. "They're building a nest for the eggs! Great huh?"

"Great," said his mother. "*Great* for you, Uncle Tano?" she asked.

"Damned great," said Tano, throwing up his hands. "Damned great!"

The three of them walked up the hill and gathered Thomas's things together. Before he zipped up his bag, Thomas opened his sketchbook to the drawing of Clara and Doc swimming in unison. It was the best drawing he had ever done. He tore it out and handed it to Uncle Tano.

The old man took the page, his hand shaking more than usual.

Then they hugged.

"Thomas is coming back this summer!" said Tano, straightening up.

"He is?" asked his mother, looking at her son. "Can I come, too?"

"Well, maybe," said Tano, looking at Thomas. "But the men in this family need some time to themselves . . . got a lot of things to do together!"

Thomas beamed and hugged the old man again.

They walked around to the front of the house, past the Chinese maple and the forsythia, now golden with blooms.

The old man stood by the car door, leaning toward the open window on the passenger side.

"Will you let me know when the goslings are born?" asked Thomas.

"Damn right, I will," said Uncle Tano, touching the boy's hair. "I sure will."

Epilogue

Thomas continued to draw. His room filled with sketches and finished drawings. His favorite was a sketch of Clara sitting on her nest on the little island. Behind her was Beauty's grave. Doc sat proudly a few feet away. Thomas made most of it up from his memories of the pond, but he was sure it was very much how the real thing would look. A month after Thomas left, Uncle Tano called to say that Clara and Doc had six goslings. He hoped that most of them would be there when Thomas came back that summer. He also told Thomas to watch out for a package in the mail. A few days later, a heavily wrapped package did come and Thomas opened it eagerly.

Inside was a small, square, stained glass panel. Thomas held it up to the light of his bedroom window. It was a glass portrait of the two geese, taken from the drawing Thomas had given Uncle Tano on his last day.

The old man had turned the black and white into radiant color. And he had changed something else. Now, the geese faced each other, beak to beak, their necks curving outward and down to their touching breasts. The shape between them looked to Thomas like a glowing blue-green heart. He wondered how the old man managed cutting such small pieces, knowing

how shaky his hands had become. As he held the panel up toward the sun, its colors fell on his face like petals of light.

Thomas propped the glass panel against his window. He thought of Luke's big, noisy, wonderful family. Yeah, he still might want to be a fifth child over there, *sometime*. But now, for the first time in his life, he felt pretty peaceful.

He felt that his family had increased by one—a big one, a crazy one, he thought smiling, but it made all the difference in the world.

Maybe he would see his father again someday. He

hoped so. He felt he had a lot to tell him, a lot to share. But best of all, Thomas felt that he had let go of a piece of himself, a piece that he didn't need to hold on to anymore, and the uncertainty of his future didn't bother him too much. Things would happen; they always did.

That night, Thomas lay awake in the dark. As his eyes closed, a "vacation" picture popped into his head. This one was different from all the others: He saw himself, his best friend Luke, and Uncle Tano shooting at tin cans by the outcropping of rocks near the woods. He could hear the buzzing of summer insects and feel the heat. Behind this laughing trio was a family of geese. A big handsome father, a one-legged mother and six midsize goslings. They were eating the grass and preening their feathers and happily making a mess on the banks of the beautiful pond.